Goodyear

THE CITY CAT

Goodyear
THE CITY CAT

Laura Jane Coats

Macmillan Publishing Company   New York
Collier Macmillan Publishers   London

Copyright © 1987 by Laura Jane Coats
All rights reserved. No part of this book may be reproduced
or transmitted in any form or by any means, electronic or
mechanical, including photocopying, recording, or by any
information storage and retrieval system, without
permission in writing from the Publisher.
Macmillan Publishing Company
866 Third Avenue, New York, NY 10022
Collier Macmillan Canada, Inc.
Printed and bound by
South China Printing Company, Hong Kong
First American Edition
10 9 8 7 6 5 4 3 2 1
The text of this book is set in 14 point Sabon.
The illustrations are rendered in watercolor
and reproduced in full color.
Library of Congress Cataloging-in-Publication Data
Coats, Laura Jane.
Goodyear the city cat.
Summary: A cat longing for adventure leaves
his comfortable home in the city and
goes in search of new experiences.
[1. Cats – Fiction] I. Title.
PZ7.C6293Go 1987 [E] 86-23782
ISBN 0-02-719051-X

In memory of
Goodyear

Goodyear was a city cat who lived in a nice apartment. He had soft pillows to sleep on, plenty of toys to play with, and a warm lap to curl up in beside the fire.

But Goodyear wasn't entirely happy. He sat at the window for hours, looking out at the world. How he longed to be in a boat on the bay.

One morning Goodyear decided he'd been in the apartment long enough. He began to work at the window latch. He pushed and pawed until finally it was free and the window swung open.

Goodyear jumped from the window to a balcony, from there to a tree, and down to the sidewalk.

Then off he went in search of adventure.

At the corner, he saw a woman knitting on a park bench. Goodyear played with her yarn and then curled up in her lap. But he didn't stay long.

He saw some children feeding ducks at a pond. One boy was sitting on the grass. Goodyear climbed into his lap and purred while the boy stroked his fur.

Next Goodyear came upon a woman selling flowers.
He jumped into her lap to smell the carnations. But
soon he was off again.

Out on a pier a man was fishing. As Goodyear watched, he pulled a fish from the water. He was too busy to have a cat in his lap.

Farther down the pier an old man was about to set sail.
"Come on board!" he called. Here, at last, was the
adventure Goodyear had been longing for.

He jumped onto the boat, and away they sailed.

All afternoon Goodyear rode up front with his paws on the railing. He could feel the sea breeze in his whiskers and the spray of the waves as the boat moved through the water.

They sailed on the bay until dusk, when the wind took
them back to the harbor.

Goodyear had a nice fish supper. Then he went to sleep in the old man's lap and dreamed of his adventurous day.

But when he awakened, the fire in the old man's stove caught his eye.

And before he knew it he was heading down the pier.

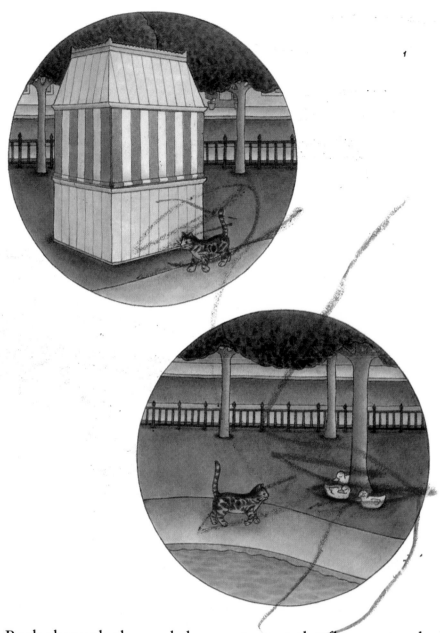

Back through the park he went, past the flower stand
and past the duck pond.

He hurried by the park bench, crossed the street, and
headed toward his apartment.

Goodyear climbed the tree and jumped to the balcony.
Then he leaped to the windowsill.

Goodyear had found lots of adventure that day and some warm laps as well. But the nicest thing he had found was that home had the lap he loved best.